DOORWAY TO DOOM

More **Strange Matter**™ from
Marty M. Engle & Johnny Ray Barnes, Jr.

DOORWAY TO DOOM

Johnny Ray Barnes, Jr.

A
MONTAGE
PUBLICATION

Montage Publications, a Front Line Company,
San Diego, California

ISBN 1-56714-063-7

Printed in the U.S.A.

TO MY WIFE, MEREDITH

Who I hope believes me when I say,
our marriage in no way inspired this title.

1

Invisible and formless, it had sensed Marge Wincott for some time, though it did not *understand* her presence. In this large, empty, office building—a place so familiar to it—Marge simply did not belong. And it wanted to know why this woman was here.

Marge typed the names across the last invitation, regretting having never learned to use a word processor.

```
        Craig and Myra Berst,
    We request your presence at our
        annual masquerade . . .
```

"Wait, it's B-U-R-S-T. *Oh my* . . ." Marge sighed, picking up the bottle of Liquid Paper

1

next to the typewriter and correcting her mistake. She was glad she had waited until after hours to type her invitations. Her co-workers would've teased her unbearably had they seen her slop the globby white paste over her misspellings.

There. Perfect. Now . . .

The fun starts at
the Wincott's
at 7:00 p.m., Octoober

"Octoober? *Oh my, not again . . .*" Marge groaned, reaching once more for the Liquid Paper.

Her hand came up empty.

She looked beside her typewriter. The little bottle was gone. She rolled back in her seat and looked down at the floor. No bottle.

She got up out of her seat and searched around her desk. She checked the wastebasket. She checked the open drawers. She checked her purse. No bottle. No bottle. No bottle.

This *could've* gotten to Marge and irritated her for hours, but she wouldn't let it—not at this late hour. The company kept more Liquid

Paper in the supply room, so she'd simply go and get more.

Marge walked through the deserted office, shutting off the lamps her co-workers had left burning at their desks. She barged into the stock room, grunting as she pushed open the heavy door.

After searching two cabinets, she found one last bottle of Liquid Paper. She grabbed and shook it.

Empty.

She frowned. Then she heard a voice whisper in her ear.

Who are you?

Marge dropped the bottle and spun around.

Shocked, she saw no one. She stared closely at the taped boxes piled against the opposite wall. Other than those, she stood alone in the tiny room.

Marge sighed and started to walk out when . . .

. . . *The heavy stock room door blew open and nearly struck her!*

Marge screamed in terror. Her joints locked as she gazed through the open doorway.

It appeared empty.

She looked at the door. Its handle had pierced one of the taped boxes and stuck there, keeping it from closing. New bottles of Liquid Paper fell from the hole in the box and bounced on the floor.

Then, through the doorway, she saw something strange: the lights on the desks—the ones she had just switched off—*were burning again*.

She sucked in a breath and withdrew further into the stock room. Her heart pounded. Her legs shook. *Someone had to be out there.*

Summoning her courage, she crept through the open doorway.

To her surprise, the room was still deserted. She found no one waiting to attack her. She found no one hiding behind the desks. She saw no movement whatsoever . . .

. . . *Until her typewriter started typing on its own.*

The keys slammed against the paper, clacking out a short message.

Marge stood still. Tears rolled down her

face as she stared at the typewriter, unable to accept what she'd just seen.

She started to back away, then heard the soft voice once again.

Read.

Marge shrieked, twirled, and desperately searched the room for an intruder. No one was there. Her eyes peered at the paper stuck in her typewriter. One line of type. A sentence.

Marge moved closer and read . . .

You are not who you are supposed to be.

Marge's lower lip quivered. The keys typed again. This time, two sentences.

You had better run.

She is coming.

A surge of fear shot through Marge and almost made her collapse. She had to get out of there. The stairwell exit in the corner of the room! She'd get away! She'd leave this building and this job and never come back!

Just as she turned, *the floor began to shake.*

Without warning, the entry door to the top floor offices burst open, and Marge Wincott erupted in shrieks.

Plaques and pictures flew off the walls and smashed to the floor. Potted plants and pencil mugs exploded by themselves, scattering fine fragments through the air. A tornado of papers blew into the room. Then the desks creaked— *just before they overturned, seemingly by themselves.*

Marge cried out against the thunderous crashings of office furniture striking the floor. An invisible bulldozer uprooted the workstations and barreled through the office—a white-desked tidalwave headed straight for the awestruck accountant.

Bawling hysterically, she shot to the stairwell exit. Flinging open the door, she bolted down the steps. The rolling herd of wood pieces crashed against the wall and stopped—but the flying papers funneled their way down the stairwell after her. They wound around the turns like a snaking twister, and Marge felt them nick her calves with their sharp corners. Her legs hammered like pistons down seven flights before she reached the bottom floor and tore into the building's lobby.

Behind her, the door swung open and smashed against the wall.

It was coming.

She ran for the glass exit doors without looking back. She held her hands in front of her, ready to crash through them if necessary. *Then the unthinkable happened . . .*

She tripped.

Marge struck the floor hard, just as a raging current of wind passed above her so fast she could feel it tug at the roots of her hair.

The plate glass window shattered, and what followed sounded like a heavy wailing moan. *Then . . .*

The sound trailed off. A quivering Marge Wincott watched the last bits of glass dangle and drop to the floor as Ivan Brewer, temporary building security man, appeared on the other side of the shattered frame with a horrified look on his face.

"MRS. WINCOTT! WH—WHAT HAPPENED?"

Marge tried to answer, but fainted instead.

Ivan raced in to help her, calling her name while reaching for his radio to call for assistance.

Behind him, the front door opened softly and *something else* left the office building, escaping into the night.

2

TWO WEEKS LATER.

"They're still out there. I know it. Hundreds of them. No, maybe thousands of them—just waiting to catch me walking down a dark secluded street at night. Or maybe stalking me, watching for that one brief moment when I'm the last one to leave school, or I'm left to wait in the car, or I'm the only one in the house. Or maybe, maybe they're still lurking in the woods . . ."

The video camera framed Fairfield—the small town basked in the warm glow of the sun. It was a perfect day to be outside enjoying the beauty of this hidden Rockwellian paradise.

Waylon Burst lowered the camera from his eye and looked through the window at his home town. His eyes flickered in apprehension.

His muscles tensed . . . in fear.

"They're out there," he whispered. "The monsters are out there."

"WAYLON! ARE YOU UP IN YOUR ROOM TALKING TO THAT VIDEO CAMERA AGAIN?" thundered a voice from downstairs.

Waylon sat in the darkness of his bedroom, looked straight at his camera, and lied.

"NO."

"WELL GET DOWN HERE, SON. YOUR NEW BABYSITTER'S GOING TO BE HERE IN A MINUTE AND YOU COULD AT LEAST MEET THIS ONE INSTEAD OF LOCKING YOURSELF IN YOUR ROOM!"

"TWO MINUTES," Waylon replied, then held down the red button on his camera.

"TWO MINUTES!" the deep voice warned.

Waylon sighed, lifted his camcorder up to the window, and recorded the last few minutes left in the day.

Downstairs, the babysitter had arrived. Eager for someone new to talk to, Mr. Burst let her in quickly and sat her down to listen to his tales. He loved to brag.

"I made my money in wrestling. Well, enough money to invest in the garage, anyway. The first twenty-four-hour garage in Fairfield. A certified success! After that, I muscled my way into other towns, opening up locations from Lake Wataga to Mullenfield. Of course, that funded the remodeling of this house, which was at first just a normal split-level. But I've made a new addition every year for the past five years, and it's becoming quite the estate, wouldn't you say . . .?"

Bonnie Roeborn patiently listened from the edge of Mrs. Burst's favorite Victorian chair. She sat hunched over—her long dirty-blonde hair fell into her nervous twitching eyes. She wore a flannel shirt because she loved the feel, and a *Foo Fighters* T-shirt because her parents hated the band. That, coupled with her faded jeans and black combat boots, hid the badge of "babysitter" very well for Bonnie. Lucky for her, she came highly recommended. Of course, Mr. Burst wouldn't know what she looked like. He'd been staring into the mirror since she'd arrived, and his stories were meant to amuse himself more than her. "Mr. Burst, where's Waylon?"

"He's doing something upstairs," he answered, running a comb through his greased-back hair. "I told him to come down and meet you. I must ask, what has my wife told you about Waylon?"

Bonnie smiled, "She told me he likes to stay in his room."

Mr. Burst turned, popped a breath mint into his mouth, and returned the smile. "That he does. But there's a reason for that. You see, Waylon . . . is *scared* to go outside."

"Why? Is someone after him?"

Surprised by her frankness, Mr. Burst's eyebrows lifted.

"Well, he thinks so. It seems that last year Waylon thought he saw something in the woods."

"What did he see?"

Mr. Burst grinned uneasily.

"Well, if you ask me, it was any number of sneaky animals you might find roaming about in the wild. But Waylon, he thinks he saw a monster."

"A monster? What kind?"

"One with red eyes, long nails, green skin, and all that—it doesn't matter. What matters is that he's barely left this house since. He hasn't gone anywhere but school or wherever his mother and I might drag him. He simply will not leave the house. Instead, he reads the books he begs me to buy or order through the mail for him. Books about strange creatures. And when he's not reading, he's watching monster videos until all hours of the morning. He draws, he writes, he devises plans against the oncoming forces of the dark unknown. At least that's what he tells me. He's not a regular boy anymore, not like he used to be."

"I heard he used to be kind of mean."

"He wasn't mean. He was a motivator. He went out and got what he wanted and encouraged others to do the same. Now, he's just pale; he needs some sun."

"So, will he give me any trouble?" Bonnie asked.

"No," said *Mrs. Burst*, coming into the room. "He'll come down and meet you, and then he'll go up to his room just like he always does. We just feel better knowing someone's here to watch him." She wore a beautiful dress from the Civil War era, one that Bonnie swore she knew from somewhere.

"Hey, you're Scarlett O'Hara, right?" Bonnie asked.

"You're half right, dear. I'm Vivian Leigh portraying Scarlett O'Hara. My husband, Craig, is Clark Gable as Rhett Butler. We always dress as a dashing Hollywood couple for Mrs. Wincott's annual masquerade. It's such a shame what happened to her."

"Yeah, my mom was . . . *working* . . . over at the Wincott's the day Mr. Wincott brought his wife home from the hospital. The doctors said she suffered from a case of collapsed nerves."

"Well, it was very nice of the Corbens to uphold the grand tradition. And in that big beautiful house of theirs . . ."

"I know. Mom cleans, um, *works* with the Corbens, too."

Mrs. Burst smiled politely, nodded, then—

"WAYLON! GET DOWN HERE AND MEET YOUR SITTER!"

As Mr. and Mrs. Burst finished making the final adjustments on their collars and sleeves, Bonnie heard a slight creak at the top of the stairs. A twisted shadow appeared on the wall at the top of the stairway and started coming down slowly, dragging itself over the carpeted steps.

Finally, the fleshy mass appeared.

Wide-eyed and pale with a slight coat of oil covering his pasty skin, he crept into the den as if he were waiting for wolves to pounce. He looked at Bonnie not with contempt, like most of her sittees did, but with fear. Total fear. He was truly scared of what Bonnie might do to him.

Thunderation, Bonnie thought.

"Bonnie, this is our son, Waylon."

3

"Hi. I'm going back up to my room now."

"WAYLON," his father started to shout, then remembered their company. "Waylon, speak to your babysitter. We're hoping to keep this one."

"Hi."

"Hi," said Bonnie noticing the camcorder in his hand. "What are you filming?"

"My room. Keeping tabs on my room," Waylon squeaked. His eyes kept darting around.

Very nervous kid, Bonnie thought. "Why are you doing that?"

"I've . . . got to get to my room now."

"*Waylon*, you'll stay down here and actually talk to another human being for five minutes. Your mother and I are leaving now. Ready, dear?"

"Yes," said Mrs. Burst, adjusting her sun bonnet one last time in the mirror. "Now Bonnie, the number to the Corbens' is listed at the bottom of Mr. Burst's address book, which is on his desk in the study. If there's any trouble, call us."

"Will do, Mrs. Burst. Have a great time," replied Bonnie.

"Thanks," answered Mr. Burst. "And Waylon, be a gentleman, *like me*." Running his hand over his slicked-back hair, he opened the door for his wife.

Bonnie held her breath until they left the driveway, her muscles relaxing as the Bursts' Mercedes disappeared at the end of the street. Then she turned around with a smile, but it quickly disappeared when she saw Waylon.

He stood motionless, staring at her as if she were sprouting wings from her back. As if horns jutted from her forehead. As if her eyes turned blood red and her teeth grew into fangs. *As if . . .*

"What is wrong with you?" Bonnie asked. "You're freaking me out!"

"Nothing. I'm going up to my room now."

Bonnie sighed. She didn't mean to be rude. This house, this huge house in which she could only dream of ever living, made her nervous. The Bursts, with their sophisticated mannerisms, overwhelmed her. And Waylon just made her nervous. But she was older than he was; she should at least act like it.

"Listen, I'm sorry. It's just, well, I've never heard of a kid who didn't like going outside. It's kind of . . . unhealthy, isn't it?"

"No."

"No? So, it's healthier to lock yourself in your room and stay inside all the time?"

"Yes."

This was getting irritating.

"Well, if it floats your boat. But do you mind if I tell you something?" She didn't wait for him to answer. "You look terrible. I mean, really bad. I'm surprised your parents haven't locked you in a hospital . . ."

"They've tried . . ."

"And your mental facilities. How can you stay in tune with reality when you're hidden away in this place," Bonnie rambled, waving her arms over the immense vastness that was the Bursts' living room. "The only you thing you do is sit on your bed and videotape your own room!"

Stunned, she shut her mouth. What had

she done? What had she been thinking? She had just completely insulted her biggest clients' kid and she hadn't even been there five minutes. She'd blown this job!

Waylon just watched her. His eyes seemed to bulge out of his head, as if making room for some of the truth Bonnie had just dished out. Then he noticed the blinking light on his camcorder; time for a recharge.

He silently walked over to the largest entertainment center Bonnie had ever seen and set the camera down next to its battery charger. He plugged it in as Bonnie began to apologize profusely . . .

"Listen, I'm sorry. Really. Please, don't tell your parents I . . . See, these babysitting jobs are really important . . . I've got a good reputation . . . if it leaks out that I actually insulted one of the kids . . ."

"I'm videotaping my room because I've been hearing noises in it for the past week. The things that are outside . . . those things have gotten in. I'm sure of it. And I'm not letting them get me. I'm videotaping my room because I'm going to find out what the things are and get rid of them. I'm not letting them get me."

With that, Waylon Burst turned and went back up the stairs. Bonnie heard a door slam, and her heart sank. She'd really done it this time. She walked over to the Victorian chair and collapsed into it, looking up at the high ceiling and the beautiful clown paintings that hung on the walls. She'd never have a house like this. Never . . .

Waylon flipped the light switch. Its circuit ran to a wall outlet plugged with a surge protector. That surge protector housed five different outlets, all of them filled with plugs. Each cord from the five plugs ran to a lamp. The first sat on the floor, an adjustable that shined brightly under his bed. The next plug ran to a halogen that sat atop his book shelf, illuminating all of the ceiling corners. A third plug was connected to a spotlight that shone on everything in his closet, from the old boxes on the top shelf to the shoe piles in the bottom corner. The last two were mounted above the doorway of his private bathroom. The lamps held back the room's darkness until Waylon could get there and flip the lights on himself.

Rigging the light system had been one of

the first things he had done. Under all of that brightness, he would sit on his bed and try to re-create on paper what he had seen in real life. The walls were covered with his drawings of red-eyed human-sized lizards, and ranged from the simple to the highly-detailed.

Shortly after he had started drawing, he had begun reading as well. In a very short time, he'd accumulated a small library of books on strange phenomena. In them, he searched for the creatures he'd seen in the woods, but to no avail. However, the stories and facts on those pages had opened up a new world to him. The more literature he consumed, the more he was convinced that the forces of darkness were out there. Waiting for Waylon Burst to step outside.

He wouldn't give them the pleasure.

Instead, he promised himself not to go outside if he could help it. Not because he was afraid, but because he was too valuable. Waylon had seen something most people hadn't. He'd looked into the blood-red eyes of hideous mon-sters and had lived. He knew that no matter what it took, he had to figure out a way to stop them before they tried to take over the world. And now *they knew* that he knew. They would send agents after him. They would employ whatever measures they had to in order to get into the house and get to Waylon. They wouldn't let him interfere with their ultimate plan to take over the world . . . small town by small town.

Waylon's eyes glanced over the bookcase, searching for tonight's lesson.

GHOSTS, SPIRITS, AND POLTERGEISTS.

The title brought on a mild shiver.

From what he'd read so far, there was no one sure-fire defense against these paranormal phenomena. *Incorporeals* is how he had best heard them described. They were intangible horrors that could be anyplace at any time. From what he had read before, the *poltergeist*s were the worst. It was practically impossible to get rid of them, and it had even been rumored that some could produce manifestations of things from their past to haunt the present. How could a person prepare for something like that?

Knowledge is my best defense, Waylon thought, pulling the book from his shelf. He laid on his bed, resting his back against the headboard, and got set to read all about awful apparitions. Without thinking, he reached over and flipped on his radio.

Every light in the room went off.

Waylon shot up—mumbling.

"With all the lights on, the radio trips the fuse. With all the lights on, the radio trips the fuse . . ."

How many times have I done it? he asked himself. The first time it happened, he'd screamed loudly enough not only to wake up his parents, but also the Reeces next door.

Waylon jumped to his feet, then caught a glimpse of something outside his window.

Something was moving.

All of the air left his lungs and he suddenly felt faint.

This is it, his mind raced.

He moved just close enough to the glass to look down into his yard and see them.

Three shadowy figures moving toward the house.

4

Thirty seconds before Waylon's blackout, Bonnie had seen something that terrified her.

It had caught her so off-guard, she had to rewind the tape to view it again.

Unable to stand the silence downstairs, she'd played Waylon's tape in the VCR. What horrified her wasn't the seemingly obsessive, mad ramblings of the videographer, but what his camera had caught.

An outline.

It was something Waylon apparently hadn't seen, because he kept going on about the terrors that awaited him in the streets. It was an outline, appearing beside Waylon's own reflection in the window glass. A small outline of . . . *it looked like* . . . To be sure, she played it one more time.

Then Waylon screamed from upstairs.

"LOCK THE DOORS. LOCK ALL THE DOORS!"

Bonnie leapt to her feet.

"WHAT?"

A loud slam came from just around the corner of the living room. From Mr. Burst's study . . .

"WAYLON—WHAT'S GOING ON?"

SLAM! The same sound again—then again. And again. The noise was unmistakable; doors were being shut.

"WAYLON, WHY ARE YOU SLAMMING THE DOORS!"

Waylon screamed down a horrifying answer—

"I'M NOT!"

"I'M CALLING YOUR PARENTS!" Bonnie screamed, and ran to the study. The study door was shut. She twisted the handle and burst into the dark room. Before she could find a light, the door closed behind her. She jetted over to it and tried to yank it open again.

It wouldn't budge.

Waylon gritted his teeth and pulled the door handle with all his might.

Nothing. The stupid door wouldn't open.

They've trapped me . . . he panicked. *They're coming, and the door won't—*

"BONNIIIIIIIIIEEEEE! HELP MEEEE!" he screamed. The intensity of his cry burned his throat. "BONNIIIEEE!"

No answer.

They have her, oh no, they have her, too!

He backed away from the entry, suddenly aware that the shadowy figures could come busting through at any second. In the darkness, he felt around for a hiding place—then was stunned by a flash of light.

Blue light. Flickering from under his bathroom door.

Oh no, oh no, oh no, oh no, oh no, oh no . . .
They're here.

💀 💀 💀

The three shadowy figures hugged the side of the house, stalking their prey who lay inside, nearly at his wit's end.

"Do you really think we'll be able to scare him?"

"Blade, I could throw a mouse in his room and the paramedics would be at the door in three minutes. I'm telling you, Waylon Burst has become a wimp."

"Wolf's right," Count Nefarious whispered. "Do you know who was picking on him the other day? Doug Lackey. Little boy Doug Lackey. Waylon wouldn't even fight back. It's embarrassing!"

"You bet it's embarrassing," Wolf fumed. "We used to follow this guy. He used to be our leader. Now he's a sniveling fraidy-cat. That makes us look bad, man."

"So why did you make me bring my camera?" asked Blade.

"Cause we're going to extract an ooo-please-don't-hurt-me-I'm-a-yellow-bellied-coward-sissy look from his face, and you'll snap the picture. His true colors will come shining through, and the whole school will see copies of it passed around. Our names will be attached to the prank, and everyone will see that we no longer have anything to do with Waylon Burst."

"But won't we get in trouble?" Blade asked.

Wolf shrugged, "You don't call yourself

'Blade' because you want the principal to like you, do you?"

While Blade shook his head, Count Nefarious asked the obvious question.

"How will we get in? You've been here more times than we have."

"Come on. I'll show you."

The three ex-henchman of Waylon Burst, former school bully, skulked silently around the home of their once-admired leader. This night had been planned for some time—their ultimate endeavor to save face. This would be the final cut that would clearly separate them from Waylon's fall from grace, and add a clever revenge tale to the trio's growing legend.

The Terrible Three. Wolf liked that name. Shapeless. Faceless. Ominous. The Terrible Three said it all. Wolf was about to suggest it to the others when he arrived at their secret entrance.

"Hmm. It's locked," said Wolf, standing beside the folding cellar doors in the back of the Burst home.

"How are we going to get in?" asked the Count.

Wolf reached into his pocket and produced

a key.

"Waylon had one made for me. In the days when it was just me and him, we'd meet down here and plan out who we were going to beat up. I just hope it still works."

Wolf wrestled the key into the chain lock and, after a couple of twists, it snapped open. He grabbed the door and pulled it out, wincing at the loud, chilling squeak it made on its way. He set the door softly to the ground, and the three of them peered into the unyielding blackness below.

"Well," said Count Nefarious, "go ahead."

Wolf turned to him and slightly grinned.

"No way, big man. I brought the key. You go down there."

The Count shook his head. "No. Nope. No way. I, sirs, will not be the first to go down there. I'm letting you fellas know that right now."

"Blade, you're the man."

"I'm the man?" Blade asked.

"Yeah. Listen. All you have to do is go down the steps, walk straight for about five feet and reach up to pull the light switch chain hanging from above. Simple as that," Wolf explained.

"If it's that simple, why don't you—"

"Blade, listen, please. It's getting late and we're all a little tired. We've come a long way and I'm sure no one here wants to go home without seeing this thing to its final conclusion. Now, this is your part in it. Go down those steps, and fulfill your duty."

Blade looked at Wolf with pleading eyes, but when Count Nefarious closed in on him, he realized his cause was hopeless. He turned to the dark void at his feet and with a long deep breath, prepared for his descent into the abyss.

From out of the blackness they sprang.

Three long, hairy arms—*one blue, one yellow, one red*.

They grabbed each boy by the shirt and pulled them into the dark dank hole.

The Terrible Three never had a chance to scream as the cellar doors slammed shut.

2

The cellar doors . . .

That sound had to be the cellar doors . . .

But if they're in the cellar, then what is this thing flashing in my bathroom?

Waylon couldn't decide.

He could stay hidden in the corner and rot, or he could get up and find answers to his questions. If something was in that bathroom, it wasn't coming out.

So Waylon made his choice. He drew in a breath and stood up, his knees popping as he reached his full height. The butterflies in his stomach turned to bats, landing on and gnawing at his inner lining. The things . . . the monsters . . . had come, and they were daring him to come out of his shell.

I've prepared for this, he thought.

Running his hand over his hardwood floor, he found the two loose boards. He lifted them and grabbed one of the numerous weapons he kept hidden all around the house. A baseball bat. He raised it into the air and approached the bathroom.

The light continued to flash underneath the door. Never once did it speed up or slow down. It just kept blinking. Waiting.

Waylon's blood froze as his sweaty palm turned the handle. The air made a small popping sound as he pushed it open . . .

The long wall. The long wall! That stupid wall that separates the bathroom from its entrance. He'd have to turn the corner to actually see what was in there.

The light strobing on the walls made the bathroom look like a discotheque. He pressed his face up against the wall, feeling its coolness as he inched to the corner . . . to the edge . . . and peeked around . . .

And screamed.

Bonnie heard him, just as she finally found the light.

Pulling the lamp string, she expected to see someone standing there in the room, waiting for her. But while Waylon was shrieking at who-knows-what upstairs, Bonnie stood alone.

Running back over to the door, she tried once again to force it open. *If she could get out of there, she could help Waylon, she could—*

The door still wouldn't budge.

Mr. Burst's address book. Bonnie raced back across the room and frantically scanned the desk for it.

A mess. She couldn't find anything under the huge pile of papers that scattered to the ground as soon as she touched it.

Forget it—I'll call 9-1-1 . . .

Snatching up the phone, her fingers punched in the numbers. She listened for the ring, but didn't hear one.

Instead, she heard what sounded like people mumbling. Hundreds of them, spouting so much gibberish that they sounded like a swarm of bees.

"HELLO?" Bonnie cried. "HELLO? CAN SOMEONE HEAR ME? I NEED HELP!"

The voices continued. A sea of murmurs.

"AARRGGHH!" she screamed, and slammed the receiver down hard enough to bust off the mouthpiece and put a dent in Mr. Burst's desk.

"Oh. *Oh gosh* . . ."

Then came a knock at the door.

"WAYLON? WAYLON IS THAT YOU?"
Silence.
"WAYLON?"

Three more knocks.

"Oh man . . ."

Bonnie gritted her teeth, grabbed the phone again, and searched around the desk for the mouthpiece. When she found it, she clumsily reattached it to the receiver and listened for a dial tone. She heard nothing.

The knocking continued without pause.

"No. Come on . . ." she whispered, punching the dial tone button again and again. There was still no sound.

"Please . . . please . . . just give me a sound . . . anything . . ."

She hit the dial tone button in rapid succession, then listened.

Nothing. Then . . .

The murmuring.

Bonnie shook her head in frustration. Tears began to well up in her eyes. This was unbelievable. Completely unbelievable.

Then suddenly, one of the voices on the phone became clear. *It asked* . . .

"Floris DeDoris, is that really you? I've been looking for you! I've been looking for Momma, too, but I can't find her. Floris is it really you?"

"Help me. Please help me! My name's Bonnie Roeburn and I'm trapped at 1705 Cleo Drive! Someone's broken into the house and I'm trapped! Please help me . . ."

Silence on the other end.

"You're not Floris DeDoris. You're an imposter. This isn't going to make G.I. Joan very happy. I sent her and the Space Ghoul to find Floris DeDoris. What, with her face having been melted and the dogs ripping her to shreds and all, she's really not going to be in the mood to find *you* there instead of her."

"What are you talking about?" Bonnie

panicked. Then, the knocking at the door turned into pounding and the walls started shaking.

"G.I. Joan is the military's very special secret weapon. A one-woman force who seeks out the enemy and brings its tyranny to an end. She's proud. She's noble. And she's reporting for duty. What's her next mission? You decide . . ."

The voice on the phone trailed off as Bonnie's heart sank. Bewildered and terrified, she couldn't think of anything to do but ask . . .

"G.I. JOAN? IS THAT YOU?"

The pounding stopped.

The handle twisted, and the door slowly creaked open.

6

Bonnie held her breath. Her blood turned to ice in her veins. Her legs begged to collapse.

The door swung all the way open revealing . . . nothing.

Bonnie blinked, then blinked again. There was nothing there. Nothing at all. It took her a moment to collect her wits.

Then she bolted for the door and slammed it shut. Breathlessly, she leaned against it and held it shut until she could think of her next move.

Nothing there. Could be a trick. I'll give it a few seconds. Nothing there—

It took a long moment of deep breathing for her to calm down the slightest bit. She clutched her chest, feeling her hammering heart slowly wind down enough for her to think rationally.

Nothing there. Nothing there.
Then she heard a scream from upstairs.
Waylon . . .

She jerked open the door, and there it stood. A seven-foot-tall hulking mass of flexing plastic with a melted head. It wore shredded green combat fatigues and a smeared half-smile. It gurgled sickly . . .

"LADY LIBERTY SHINES!"

. . . And grabbed Bonnie by the throat. With not so much as a grunt, it lifted her into the air. Bonnie couldn't scream. It was so disgusting, she thought she might get sick—

This thing's face was like a fashion doll's—but pushed in on one side as if the air had been sucked from her head. The other side was a mess of melted facial features. Her hair had been ripped from her forehead, leaving holes in her scalp. Instead, her long blonde mane, frizzed and blown, began in the middle of her head. The olive military gear she wore was ripped and torn. G.I. Joan had been chewed and gnawed on—drenched in saliva then spit out.

"GGNNNGGGHHH—" Bonnie struggled. *WHAT IS THIS? WHAT IS THIS THING? HOW CAN IT BE ALIVE?* she thought.

Bonnie grabbed the thing's wrist in a vice grip. There was an audible "pop", and Bonnie fell to the floor with the hand still around her neck. She felt the end of it, where the wrist used to be, but now there was a . . . *ball joint?*

"Oohh, noo . . . "

💀 , 💀 💀

Waylon couldn't believe it.

He had turned the corner and now saw something in his shower. Something behind the distorted mosaic design in the glass shower doors. He could only make out a form. It stood with its arms bent and held up in the air. It was primarily blue, and undoubtedly the source of the light that had washed over his bathroom. And it was making an awful squishing noise.

Waylon's nerves huddled. His throat swelled, ready to scream, but a witless, despicable emotion held it back. Fear. The fear of not knowing who or what it could be. The fear of it never leaving. The fear of it coming back. He couldn't leave it like this. He had to put a face on the terror that fed on his heart.

With a shaking hand, he pulled the shower door open.

That's when he screamed the second time.

It . . . it was horrible.

In his shower stood something close to human. Something from outer space. Clad in a white, skin-tight, diving suit, wrapped in a baggy, clear, plastic coating. It wore heavy white gloves and boots and a glass bubble helmet on top of its head. Its face—a skull—covered by taut white skin. It had eyes. Bulging white eyes with pulsing red veins. And it glowed. The whole thing glowed as it held its arms bent upwards . . . and waited. A digital display on its chestplate read: **RE-ENERGIZING**.

That's where the squishing came from—a tube running from the middle of the suit to the shower faucet. It pumped something . . . nasty . . . into the suit. Grainy blue jelly. The tube contracted and lengthened as it pumped the stuff into the suit.

A sick feeling rushed up from Waylon's stomach, but recoiled when he saw the thing's eyes turn to look at him. It stepped out of the shower and came toward him. Its chestplate reading: **RESUME SEARCH**.

Waylon raced for the door and found it closed. He grabbed the handle. He pulled. He yanked. It wouldn't open.

The pumping noise got louder. The ghoulish spaceman walked toward him, its hands out and its jaw dropped. The lumpy jelly filled the clear bubble lining of its suit, packing it and making it bulge. Its entire body glowed now, and it cracked a sickening laugh as it came closer.

7

Waylon kicked and tore at the door with madness in his eyes. The veins in his temples threatened to burst and his tongue quivered with the scream that tried to jump out.

But the thing had reached him.

Waylon crumpled to the ground and held his hands in the air as a desperate last defense.

Then the thing stopped.

Its tube stretched tight, keeping it from going any farther. The filthy gelatin still poured into the suit, which had by now ballooned to optimum capacity. When the thing stepped back, the weight of the suit made it lose its balance, and the monster fell to the ground.

Waylon watched it land on its back, then struggle as it grew larger, unable to get up. Squishing. Expanding.

Waylon could see the inevitable coming and screamed. He pulled and tore at the door, but it wouldn't budge.

The ghoul gurgled and kicked under the incredible pressure until it could do so no more. The plastic film stretched as tight as it possibly could.

Then it exploded.

Waylon felt his mouth fill with goo as jelly flew everywhere, covering the walls and the mirrors, the tub and the floor, flying in Waylon's eyes, ears, nose, and hair. The horrible, greasy, gelatinous slime lined every inch of the bathroom, and dripped from every tile. Waylon quivered in revulsion.

The ghoul still moved. It kicked its legs in in the air and waved its arms, almost like a newborn infant.

Waylon got to his feet and looked down at it. The bulging white eyes sank down in their sockets, and then the monster ceased to move.

The door behind Waylon creaked open. He whipped around in shock expecting to see some other terror standing there, but it was clear.

Waylon took a last look at the bubbling monstrosity on his bathroom floor and then crept out. The door slammed behind him. Unnerved, he gripped the handle and opened it again.

Empty. The entire bathroom was semi-clean and free of blue ooze, just as it was before the thing had appeared. As if the encounter had never happened.

Then he saw a blue light. Turning around, he saw it flickering under his closet door, begging him to have a look.

"Not in a million years," Waylon gasped, and darted for his bedroom door. He pulled on it. Still stuck.

Then behind him, he heard a scraping sound. *Something was carving into wood . . .*

He turned to see words being cut into his closet door, forming a question:

WHO ARE YOU?

"Who am I? WHO AM I?" he screamed. "WHO ARE YOU?!" he asked back. Suddenly the door to his room creaked open. He shot out without thinking, and instead of the floor, his feet met something thin and flimsy.

"NO! ACCH—" he turned back for his

bedroom door, but it closed too fast. He tried to open it. Locked again.

"Oh, man . . . what now . . .?"

His hallway had turned to cardboard. From ceiling to floor and wall to wall, solid surfaces were now made of moving-box material. Stepping lightly on it, there seemed to be nothing underneath it to brace it. He pushed the wall and it crinkled and bent. It reminded him of . . .

Something moved from around the corner at the end of the brown hallway. Waylon jerked around, his eyes wide.

He hoped, and called out.

"BONNIE?"

💀   💀   💀

"NO!" Bonnie cried, lunging for the desk as G.I. Joan swung Mr. Burst's American flag at her.

"I DO IT ALL FOR MOTHER AMERICA!"

Bonnie clumsily slid over the desk, sending papers and books flying into the air and onto the floor. She flew over Mr. Burst's chair and flipped onto the carpet. Mr. Burst's thick address book lay beside her head. She looked up and grabbed the book just in time to block the end of the flagstaff. G.I. Joan grunted and tried to force it through the address book. Bonnie tossed the book, crawled under the desk, and ran to the door.

"YOU CAN'T TREAD ON AMERICA'S BEAUTY!"

With incredible precision, G.I. Joan thrust the staff through the air like a javelin. It speared the door just as Bonnie closed it on her way out, the address book still stuck on its tip.

Outside the study, Bonnie tripped, got back up, and bolted for the front door. *She'd call the police to come help Waylon. He was a smart kid. He could stay alive until then.* When she reached the door . . .

"OH, BIG SURPRISE."

Locked.

Slumping in dread, she peeked over her shoulder toward Mr. Burst's study. The door remained closed.

She listened for a noise. She wanted to hear a crack, a thud, a shift in the air—anything to warn her of an attack. She heard nothing, except . . .

Screaming. Wails of terror. Coming from somewhere in the distance—but close.

She crept across the room, never taking her eyes off of the study door, but zeroing in on the screaming. It seemed to come from the kitchen.

Bonnie plunged her hand into the dark room, feeling the wall for a light switch. When she found one, she flipped it on, exposing the blue, green, and yellow flowered walls and the white countertops of the Burst kitchen.

She mustered some courage and stepped in, listening to the muffled shrieks and cries that grew louder with each step. She looked under the white-tiled breakfast table, over the spotless counter, and even in the stainless steel oven before she stopped—right in front of the refrigerator.

Breath held, she opened it.

A tangled mess of arms erupted from the fridge, reaching out for something to grab.

Bonnie shrieked and jumped back against the cabinet door behind her.

Blue furry arms, red furry arms, yellow furry arms, and even fleshy arms stretched to full extension, grabbing each other as well as the door shelf condiments. She couldn't get past them to get away. Trapped and terrified, she peered into the refrigerator.

Monkeys. Blue, red, and yellow monkeys. There must've been twenty of them rolling around in there. And they had the longest arms she'd ever seen. The swirling simians shrieked and squealed and laughed—but didn't scream.

"HELP ME! GET ME OUT OF HERE!" cried the bouncing head of a young boy inside. *He* was screaming.

8

"PLEASE HELP ME!" cried the terrified face.

The kid pushed and climbed through the rolling monkeys, toward the refrigerator doorway and managed to shove his hand out. With more courage than she thought she had, Bonnie grabbed it and pulled the boy out of the crashing wave of monkeys.

"PULL HARDER! I'VE GOT FRIENDS IN HERE!"

Bonnie's eyes widened as she heaved. Moving into the center of the kitchen, she hauled three boys out of the monkey-filled refrigerator, all of them linked by tightly-clutched hands. As soon as the last boy pulled free, he slammed the door closed with his foot . . . and then started kicking it.

"STAY IN THERE YOU STUPID MON-

KEYS! STAY IN THERE AND CHILL!"

"STOP IT!" cried Bonnie. "STOP KICKING THE REFRIGERATOR!"

All three of the boys looked at her for a second, then got to their feet and ran out of the kitchen. She knew where they were going.

Exhausted, she returned to the living room where she found the three refrigerator escapees pulling at the front door.

"Forget it. It's locked. I've tried!"

The tallest boy gawked at her, walked over to one of the beautiful brass lamps sitting on one of the end tables and picked it up.

"Have you tried breaking a window?" he asked.

"No."

The boy swung the lamp back and hurled it at the front window. It struck the glass and . . . nothing.

"It didn't even scratch the glass," said the roundest of the boys.

"WE NEED TO THROW MORE STUFF!" yelled the shortest of the three. Then they all picked up random objects from various parts of the room and flung them at the window. Household items pummeled the glass from all directions, but it never even chipped. The boys kept throwing things until the carpet was covered with projectiles, and then dropped to the floor to catch their breaths.

"WHO ARE YOU?" Bonnie asked.

"I'm Wolf, this is Blade, and that tall guy is Count Nefarious. We're the Terrible Three."

Blade and Count Nefarious looked at him. The new title was news to them.

"You're what? How did you get in the refrigerator?" she asked, pacing the room in search of another exit.

"The monkeys pulled us in there," said Blade.

"We were cutting through the yard. We passed the cellar doors in the back and those long-armed monkeys burst out of them and grabbed us. We were yanked into a swirling pool of the things. Monkeys rolling over monkeys. It was crazy," explained Wolf.

The Count was fed up with all of this talking. "Is there any other way out of here?" he asked. "Breaking a window isn't working."

"I—" Bonnie started, then heard another scream. Muffled again, but it kept going on and on. A terrified howl coming from somewhere close.

"What's that?" Blade asked as each member of the Terrible Three got to his feet.

Bonnie knew.

Waylon.

💀 💀 💀

"WHAAAAAT'S GOOINNG OOONNN?!" Waylon screamed, jetting down the cardboard hall at full terrified speed.

He turned a corner, lost his footing, stumbled, got up, and shot away just as it poured from around the turn.

A giant blanket.

An unstoppable rolling wave of giant patchwork blanket thundering through the brown tunnel like a rushing flood. Stitched and deadly, the amoeba-like homecraft came after Waylon, winding through every twist and turn.

Waylon bolted through the thin, unstable maze, searching high and low for an escape. He'd seen no doors or windows. Just tunnel after tunnel constructed of cardboard. It reminded him of a poor man's playland—the kind of kingdom he used to build when he was just a kid. *Except his hadn't been so indestructible.*

These walls *felt* flimsy, but he'd tried to

tear through them and they wouldn't rip. Unless he found some other opening, he was trapped. Blanket prey.

He passed under a hole in the ceiling. A cardboard ductway leading up. He had to try it.

Leaping into the air, he threw his hands up and . . . HANDHOLDS! Those marvelous holes punched in the side of boxes to make lifting them easier—this tunnel had them, making climbing easier!

Not wasting a second, he pulled himself up, lifting his legs up and into the ceiling, bracing himself in the shaft just as the blanket flooded through the pathway below him.

Waylon held his breath and didn't make a sound. Beneath him, the blanket stopped flowing and turned into a pool. It rippled in hesitation, wondering where its prey had gone. Waylon called on every last ounce of self control to stay silent. To not flinch. To not crack.

His foot slipped. His foot slipped and he almost dropped right into the quilted killer. But, at the last second, he dug in and hung there for dear life.

This caught the blanket's attention.

"AWWW, CRUD . . ." Waylon exclaimed, as

the crazed covering curled then shot up into the shaft after him. It hit and pushed, and Waylon rode the bulleting blanket up the dark tunnel.

Then he hit cardboard, slamming into it face-first. The blanket kept pushing, with every intention of crushing Waylon against the thin yet impenetrable surface.

Waylon kicked and thrashed and tried to crawl out of the blanket's trap. He managed to turn his head and saw . . .

Light! The blanket had pushed him into a turn in the tunnel. The shaft continued to the right, and there was light shining at the end of it! *And light means something other than card-board!*

These facts squeezed together in Waylon's brain as the blanket applied more pressure to his head against the cardboard. He felt his eye-balls grow larger, ready to pop out of his head. He curled into a ball—positioning his feet for one last desperate attempt at escape.

Then he went wild—wrestling and punching until he gained enough leverage to pull himself free and crawl down the shaft—toward the light.

Surprisingly, the shaft was slanted.

Rolling down the duct head over heels, he had no way of stopping or even slowing down before he went into the light, hit something, and burst through.

He saw light. He saw carpet. He saw black.

Then he saw Bonnie's face. She held his head in her hands, and suddenly started shaking him furiously.

"WHAT'S GOING ON IN THIS HOUSE?" she screamed in his face. "WE CAN'T GET OUT! WE CAN'T CALL ANYONE TO GET US OUT! YOU'D BETTER TELL ME WHAT'S GOING ON IN THIS HOUSE!"

She dropped his head and waited for an answer. Waylon shook the rattles out of his skull, saw the Terrible Three standing over him, and then shook the rattles some more. He got to his feet and looked around.

Plain white walls. Yellow-tiled floor. Bad dog art on the walls. They were in the laundry room.

"How'd I get here?" Waylon asked.

"We heard you screaming," said Bonnie. "We followed your high-pitched wails here, then you fell out of that cabinet." She pointed to the cabinet on the wall where Waylon's mom kept all the detergents. "Now listen, Waylon. I'm not blaming you or anything, but things just seem a little too coincidental here. I mean, you're always looking for monsters, right? Well, tonight your house is full of weird stuff like that. I'm asking you if you have any idea what's going on."

Waylon rubbed his pounding head, sheepishly eyeing the four faces staring back at him.

"Yeah. I think it's a poltergeist."

9

"Will these people even know what a poltergeist is?" asked Mr. Wincott, making a final
effort to reason with his wife before she stepped
out of the car. "I mean, we invite them to the
masquerade every year, but the Bursts have
never been known as down-to-earth people.
They're pretty lofty and high-falutin'. Not really
receptive to other people's ideas!"

Marge Wincott said nothing at first, but
simply opened the door, got out, and stood in front
of the Bursts' home. Not wanting to leave the
matter unfinished, she turned to her husband.

"If these people aren't warned, what happened to me might happen to them. Or even
worse. This house holds a stronger emotional
bond with our . . . *phenomenon*. You've been
privy to all the information I have. You know

what this thing could do!"

Mr. Wincott couldn't argue with that. He'd read unbelievable reports in the case files. On the videotapes, he'd seen the rattled eyewitnesses who had broken into tears when asked to recount their experiences. He knew more about the fantastic phenomenon than he ever cared to know.

"At least let me come in there with you," he said, leaning over the seat to look at her. She had gotten thinner and her face had become more drawn over the last two weeks. The incident had really taken its toll on her.

"No, Milton. You're too edgy. You'll just make everybody nervous. Besides, you have just enough time to pick up my nerve medication at the pharmacy. When you come back, I'll be ready to go."

Mr. Wincott bit his lip, looked straight ahead, then back at his wife.

"Be careful. I'll watch you go up," he said. She responded with a smile.

He watched his beloved as she made her way to the front door and rang the bell. He never dreamed he'd be doing anything like this: actually warning a family that their house might be haunted. It was crazy. Definitely not the typical behavior of a serious bank manager like himself. But after his wife had recovered from unconsciousness in the hospital, he had vowed to do whatever he could from that day forward to make her happy. He just never imagined tracking down poltergeists would be part of it. At least it was keeping his mind off the Corbens' party. A travesty; *no one could throw a party like the Wincotts* . . .

He watched her at the door for a few more seconds until it opened. His wife slowly walked inside.

With a deep sigh, Mr. Wincott drove off, leaving his wife to warn the Bursts . . .

But no one had answered the door for her. It had opened by itself.

She stepped in carefully and saw the broken and scattered items strewn about the floor. Damaged lamps, broken vases, shattered crystal—what had happened here? Could it have been—?

"Oh. Oh, no . . .," Mrs. Wincott muttered at the thought.

The kids came into the room. Their eyes widened at the sight of Mrs. Wincott and the front door closing behind her.

In a pack, they dashed for it. Jumping over chairs and climbing over the sofa, they made a mad rush to grab the door before it closed.

Wolf had the best shot. He launched off the back of the couch, sailed into the air, flew right by Mrs. Wincott, soared over the shattered crystal and porcelain, and landed at the edge of the doorway just as the door slammed tight. He came so close that he felt a puff of air on his hand as it shut.

Before anyone could say a word, Mrs. Wincott had to know . . .

"IT'S HERE! IT'S ALREADY HERE, ISN'T IT?" she demanded.

"What?" Bonnie replied. She wanted answers. She wanted reassurance. "WHAT'S HERE?"

"THE POLTERGEIST!" Mrs. Wincott cried, then crumpled. "The poltergeist. Is it here?"

Bonnie and the Terrible Three looked at Waylon, whose face grew pale upon hearing her terrifying confirmation.

"Yes," Waylon's voice scratched. "It's here."

10

"SO WHAT DID YOU DO, WAYLON? What could you possibly have done to bring a poltergeist here?" Bonnie asked.

"I . . . don't know. I never expected it," he said, starting to feel faint as he took a seat on the couch.

"Well, Mr. Monster Magnet, how about telling me what a poltergeist is. Some of us might not be as scared of these things as you seem to be, and I'd like to know what it is I'm fighting!" demanded Wolf.

Waylon looked at him with exhaustion in his eyes.

"Where did you come from?" Waylon asked the mini-bully. Before Wolf could answer, Mrs. Wincott interrupted.

"Poltergeists are the physical activities of

ghosts directed solely by outside entities no longer in the flesh," remarked Mrs. Wincott, rendering all the kids speechless. "This link between the physical energies of living persons and the usually demented minds of dead persons produces the physical phenomena known as poltergeist activities . . ."

Waylon knew the definition and joined in.

"Which can be very destructive, sometimes threatening, sometimes baffling to those who do not understand the underlying causes," they finished reciting together. Waylon almost smiled, saying "Hans Holtzer. *Haunted America.* None of his cases resembled anything like this, though."

The rest of the kids looked at each other uneasily. Waylon and Mrs. Wincott seemed to be talking shop, and none of them were in the business.

"So a ghost is doing all of this?" Blade asked. "I thought ghosts just appeared at the tops of stairways and floated around and stuff."

"A poltergeist is focused enough to actually cause manifestations," said Mrs. Wincott.

"But you haven't seen the things that have happened in this house tonight," said

Waylon. "I've never read a case like it. This must be the most powerful poltergeist ever encountered. Where could something like this come from?"

"The underlying cause, you mean?" asked Mrs. Wincott. "Well, I think I can help you there. Ever since my . . . incident two weeks ago, I've been researching what could have possibly caused it. Since no one really believed me, I had to rely on myself. Considering the nature of the phenomenon, I came to the conclusion that it must be some kind of entity, and its questions and statements were to let me know it wants something."

"QUESTIONS?" Bonnie and Waylon chimed in at the same time. "What kind of questions?"

"It asked me, 'WHO ARE YOU?'" Mrs. Wincott answered.

"It asked me the same thing!" responded Waylon. "It carved it into my closet door upstairs."

"Well, it asked me if I was Floris DeDoris," said Bonnie, as everyone turned to look at her with questioning faces. "What? It did!"

Mrs. Wincott continued. "It also told me that I wasn't who I was supposed to be. Now, this led me to believe that this entity wanted to find someone else, but I was there instead. I'm in charge of employment records at the office. It occurred to me to go through them and find out who sat at my desk and used that rickety old typewriter before me."

"Did you—"

"Yes, a woman by the name of Millie Wall. I took this name straight to the Hall of Records here in town. It seems that Mrs. Wall had a great tragedy in her life and that's why she and her husband left town."

"What happened?" Count Nefarious asked, ready to sit and listen.

"They had a daughter named Lillian. Lillian and another child were hit by a bus," Mrs. Wincott said sadly.

"Yeah? And?" Wolf urged. Bonnie shot an elbow into his side.

"Well, I believe that's who the poltergeist is. Lillian. You see, the Walls used to live in this very house, long before your father built these, um . . . *marvelous* additions, Waylon."

Waylon stayed silent, trying to believe it . . .

"I think she has some unfinished business here," Mrs. Wincott finished.

"Like what?" Waylon asked.

"We'll have to ask her, I'm afraid. I wanted time to bring in a professional, but it looks like we'll have to contact her ourselves."

Bonnie almost snickered. "Well, you don't need a seance or anything like that. Just open any door!"

"What do you mean?" Mrs. Wincott asked.

"Well, every time you open a door, something happens. As long as you don't open one, you're safe. My guess is she's hiding somewhere behind one of the doors in this house."

Waylon's eyes suddenly widened, and he practically whispered.

"I think I know where she is. That was Lillian, in my closet . . ."

"Then let's go see if we can talk to her," Mrs. Wincott said, getting out of her seat and putting on a brave front for the children.

The kids simply watched her but didn't move.

"It's our only chance," Mrs. Wincott remarked. "If we don't, things can only get worse!"

Suddenly the kids moved. They went up the stairs in single file, with Waylon leading the way.

Things can get worse indeed, thought Mrs. Wincott. *If my suspicions are correct, Lillian may be the smallest of our worries . . .*

But she wouldn't tell the children . . . yet.

11

The group stopped just outside Waylon's room. Waylon clutched the doorknob, ever hesitant.

"Go ahead," Mrs. Wincott whispered. "Open it."

"That's easy for you to say," Bonnie remarked.

Waylon grimaced, then turned the knob and opened the door. He held his head down, eyes shut, until he heard the swinging door bump the wall. He looked up slowly.

There was his room just as he had left it—without the living monsters and stuff. Semi-clean. Very silent.

"I don't like this," commented Wolf.

Waylon froze at the doorway, unable to enter. His sanctuary—his private fortress—had been penetrated. There was nowhere safe to hide now. The monsters had come.

"GET IN THERE!" Wolf said, and pushed his former leader into the room.

Waylon whirled around and glared at him. He knew how his former henchmen felt about him. He knew that he was no longer an icon worthy of fear or even respect. But pushing him into that room where anything could happen went beyond being cruel. It was inhumane.

Waylon took a step toward the little worm, then stopped.

"What're ya gonna do, Burst?" Wolf teased. "Nothing, that's what. You lost your nerve a long time ago!"

Bonnie grabbed Wolf and threw him against the wall, knocking the Burst family portrait off the wall.

"Take it somewhere else, squirt!" Bonnie warned.

Mrs. Wincott moved between them.

"CHILDREN. We don't have time for this. We must concentrate on the task at hand—"

"Uh, Mrs. Wincott . . ." Waylon called, and the group looked into the room.

A light emanated from under the closet door, growing brighter by the second. Waylon looked at the door, then at Mrs. Wincott, and then pointed at the closet door.

Mrs. Wincott nodded and walked into the room, followed by the other four. The light danced at their feet, but there was no sound from inside the closet. Everyone felt a strong obligation to maintain the silence.

Finally Bonnie asked, "Should we see who's here?"

Waylon looked at Bonnie and Mrs. Wincott, and swallowed hard. They weren't moving. He knew what that meant; *his* closet, *he* gets to open it.

His hand practically dripped with sweat as he held on to the doorknob, turned it, and heard the door click open.

Light burst into the room as if a nuclear bomb had erupted in the closet. It practically blinded everyone.

Waylon's eyes strained to find an image. Anything to let him know what was about to destroy him.

Then he saw it, emerging from the blinding rays . . .

Oh, no . . .

12

It was one of the Friendly People.

A giant, wooden, flesh-colored ball with a simplistic human face (two black dots for the eyes, a triangle for the nose and a semi-circle for the mouth), set atop a green wooden cylinder which represented a body. Waylon recalled it from his earliest memories. One of the toys he had found in his room when they first moved in the house. Someone had left it behind. . . .

The giant wooden figure approached the group, which was too dumbstruck to even *think* of running.

"HI THERE! MIGHT I ASK YOUR NAMES?" it asked, its deep tone reverberating.

In other words, WHO ARE YOU? The same question, Waylon thought. *This poltergeist really wants an answer!*

"My name is Waylon Burst!" he exclaimed. "I live here."

The Friendly Person turned and looked around the room, almost as if it was awaiting orders.

"YOU SEE, LILLIAN WANTS TO LEAVE THIS PLACE. SHE NO LONGER FEELS AT HOME HERE. BUT BEFORE SHE LEAVES, SHE WANTS FLORIS DEDORIS."

"WHO IS FLORIS DEDORIS?" Bonnie demanded.

"I'M SO HAPPY YOU ASKED. FLORIS DEDORIS IS HER FAVORITE DOLL. BUT UNFORTUNATELY, IT HAS BEEN TAKEN FROM HER AND HIDDEN."

"WHERE?" Mrs. Wincott asked.

"WHY, THERE," said the Friendly Person, leaning toward the doorway behind them because he couldn't point.

The group turned toward Waylon's bathroom, only it wasn't Waylon's bathroom anymore. It was . . .

"Why, that's someone's garage!" exclaimed Mrs. Wincott. "Wait. I recognize the truck parked in there. That's Gene Corben's truck! That's his garage!"

"LILLIAN HAS OPENED A DOORWAY TO THE CORBENS' HOUSE. FLORIS DEDORIS IS LOCATED SOMEWHERE IN THEIR LOVELY HOME. SHE'S PROBABLY HIDDEN AWAY IN THIS GARAGE OR IN ONE OF THE ROOMS ON THE TOP FLOOR," explained the Friendly Person.

"How do you know that?" asked Bonnie.

"And why doesn't Lillian get Floris herself?" demanded Waylon.

"SORRY, GUYS. LILLIAN *CANNOT* GO THERE. SHE NEEDS SOMEONE TO GET HER DOLL FOR HER."

Wolf's wheels were turning as Mrs. Wincott spoke up.

"We want to know why she can't go there."

The Friendly Person's head turned to her.

"LILLIAN CANNOT GO THERE . . ."

Wolf interrupted.

"We'll go. We, the Terrible Three. We're the bravest ones here, anyway. We'll get the doll and bring it back, and then this whole mess will be done with."

"I don't trust you," said Waylon.

"Yeah. We'll all go," said Bonnie.

"I'M AFRAID LILLIAN WOULD LIKE

YOU TO STAY, YOUNG LADY," said the Friendly Person.

"What? Why?" Waylon asked.

"I'M NOT AT LIBERTY TO SAY . . ."

"SPILL!" demanded Bonnie.

"I'M AFRAID I CANNOT SPILL."

Then a light flashed in the hallway outside Waylon's bedroom, and a giant, plump child's hand reached into the room and grabbed Bonnie.

Screaming maniacally, she kicked and hit and punched at the hand, but it wouldn't let her go. The others joined in, but it still didn't release her. As quickly as it came, the hand pulled back out and disappeared in a cloud of dust with Bonnie tight in its grasp. The door slammed shut.

"WHERE IS SHE? WHERE DID IT TAKE HER?" Waylon yelled.

"IF YOU WOULD LIKE TO KNOW," the Friendly Person said with a stone face, "PLEASE FOLLOW ME."

A bolt of electrical fear surged through Waylon's veins. He froze at the very thought of going back through any of those doors.

"Don't worry, Waylon," Mrs. Wincott said, handing him her purse. "I'll go."

"I'M AFRAID YOU CAN'T," said the Friendly Person. "ONLY YOUNG WAYLON IS INVITED."

Everyone looked at Waylon and waited for him to make the next move.

Waylon turned to the Terrible Three and said, "Get the doll. And please, come back. We're counting on you."

"Smart guy," Wolf grinned. "Come on, Mrs. Wincott. You can go through the other door with Blade, the Count, and me. You'll be safe at the Corbens'."

Mrs. Wincott shook her head. "I can't leave the house with these children in jeopardy. I'm going to stay here and do what I can," she said, then gazed upon Waylon, who turned grimly to the Friendly Person.

"ARE WE READY?" Friendly asked.

Waylon nodded.

"LET'S BE OFF THEN," it said, and walked with Waylon into the light of the closet. The glow from the other side went super-bright, and then the door closed behind them.

Mrs Wincott and the Terrible Three stared at the closet door for a moment, then Mrs. Wincott turned to the boys.

"If I were you," Wolf said, "I wouldn't try opening any of these doors."

Then he, Blade, and Count Nefarious stepped through the door into the Corbens' garage, and the passage closed behind them.

13

"Whoa." said Blade. "We're really here."

The Corbens' garage. A dark, dusty tomb of nostalgia and a new black Ford Ranger that filled most of the space. Blade ran his fingers along the old Coca-Cola poster that hung in the window of the entry door.

"This must have been where we came in," Blade said. Holding his breath, he reached down and opened it. Nothing but backyard on the other side.

"Yep," said Wolf, "and that's exactly where we're leaving."

The Count and Blade looked stunned.

"You mean we're not going to try to find this doll?" Blade asked.

"Why should we? Let them deal with this mess! It's not our problem!"

The other two simply stared at him.

"Come on, Blade," said the Count. "Let's go find this doll."

"YOU'RE ACTUALLY GOING TO DO IT?" Wolf yelled. Then a door on the other side of the garage opened, and through it stepped something . . . not human.

It had a green head and tremendous yellow eyes with blood-red pupils.

It spoke with a heart-stopping growl.

"WHO'S OUT HERE?"

💀 💀 💀

"I know you're somewhere, I heard you!"

Nothing, not a sound. Then—

"HUSH UP, JUNIOR," growled a voice.

The light started to dim and Waylon could see something huge coming at him. Before he could get out of the way, it drove up beside him.

It was the Friendly Person, only now he didn't look so friendly (arched lines for brows, square teeth showing, painted whisker stubble on his face), and he was driving a pink, plastic, convertible Volkswagen Beetle—with purple flowers on it.

"HOP IN, FRAIDY BOY," the Friendly

Person grunted.

"But—"

"GET IN!"

"Okay, okay. Boy have you changed," muttered Waylon, trying to open the door. The latch wouldn't budge, so he just hopped into the passenger seat.

"LET'S DRIVE, FASHION BUG," the Friendly Person demanded. The car horn made an eerie sound as they sped off through the mist.

"Where are we going, Friendly Person?"

"MANNY," he growled. Then, for the first time, his voice lowered an octave. "My name's Manny. I'm only 'Friendly Person' when I'm doing delegate work for the boss, like I was out there with you and the others. Sorry about not letting the old lady come with you, but this is definitely a young person's gig, you know. There'll be running, jumping, and fighting for your life with monsters and such."

"MONSTERS? What are you talking about?"

"Well, Waylon, the boss doesn't know you're here. I stuck my, er, neck out and brought you here myself. You're going to save us, pal."

"Save you and . . . who else? How?"

"Waylon, our boss, Lillian, doesn't understand everything about being a poltergeist. The things you kids encountered tonight—the Space Ghoul, the Barrel of Laughing Monkeys, G.I. Joan—they're all things that Lillian had when she was alive. Including me and Fashion Bug here. We're the memories of those cherished childhood possessions. But see, in this existence, we're not her toys anymore. We're her soldiers. None of us want to be soldiers, except maybe G.I. Joan, and she just got replaced."

"By whom?"

"Who do you think?"

"BONNIE?"

"Yeah. G.I. Joan was Lillian's protector, but Lillian saw how Bonnie got the best of her and escaped. So now she's replaced G.I. Joan with Bonnie."

"She can do that?"

"You don't get it, Waylon. She can do *anything* here."

The mist had completely lifted. In front of the speeding Fashion Bug stood the greatest monument Waylon had ever seen.

A cardboard palace, dark, tall, and threatening—standing high against the backdrop of an inky black night. A full moon lit the hulking fortress for Waylon's wide eyes.

"Oh . . . my . . . gosh . . ."

"Massive, isn't it? See, Lillian used to build cardboard forts to play in. That's what she modeled her city after."

"So that's where I was when I got chased by the blanket."

"THE BLANKET? You got that close?"

"What do you mean 'that close'?"

"Well, none of us unhappy 'happy' memories can get close enough to Lillian to convince her to give up this useless haunting. It's not getting *her* or *us* anywhere. But she stays hidden. In the past, she was most closely guarded by G.I. Joan. The blanket was her second line of defense."

"What was her first?"

"Monsters, my friend. Hideous Monsters."

14

"That's why you're here," explained Manny. "If we can get you past those monsters and the blanket, you'll have the best chance to get by your pal, Bonnie. Then we can end this whole mess."

"What about this Floris DeDoris stuff? If Wolf, Blade, and Count Nefarious bring back the doll, then all this will end anyway, right?"

"I wouldn't count on them bringing back the doll."

"Why?"

"For the same reason Lillian won't venture into the house to get the doll herself. **Margot.**"

"**Margot?** Who's **Margot?**"

"The other girl who was hit by the bus that day was Margot. Margot's a bully. Lillian was chasing her that day because Margot stole her toy."

"Floris DeDoris?"

"No, another one. A nameless one. Margot had already taken Floris DeDoris earlier that week and hidden it in her own house."

"Her house? You mean . . ."

"Yep. Before the Corbens moved in, Margot's family lived there."

🕱 🕱 🕱

"WHO IS THAT?" the green-headed monster asked. "WHO'S BEHIND MY TRUCK?"

It was Mr. Corben—in a mask!

The Terrible Three knew they were caught. Blade sighed and stood up before the others could stop him.

"We weren't doing anything wrong, sir. We just heard the music you have playing and thought we'd see what was going on. My name's Blade, and these are my friends Wolf and Count Nefarious."

"Blade? Wolf? Count Who? Boys, those are awful names. I'm sorry for you, but please, get away from my truck. If you want to hear the music, come inside for a second and we'll call your parents," said Mr. Corben.

The boys slowly made their way around the truck and into the house. Something clicked in Count Nefarious' head as he looked at Mr. Corben's mask.

"Oh yeah, I completely forgot—*it was changed this year*. The masquerade's not at the Wincott's. It's here," remarked the Count, showing his previously unknown familiarity with Fairfield's social calendar.

The Terrible Three walked into a house filled with multi-colored streamers, loud music, and wall-to-wall laughter and conversation.

The masquerade was in full swing.

The Bride of Frankenstein stood in the kitchen filling a large silver tray with bite-sized sausage treats. George Washington walked in slowly, holding his stomach and laughing hysterically while the Hunchback of Notre Dame followed him in saying, "Let me tell you another one."

The lesser-known Squid Man of Chattanooga came into the room and made a face that said—*kids at the party? Yuck.*

"Hey, what are those kids doing here?" he asked.

"These gentlemen were about to call their

parents," said Mr. Corben, leading them to a phone sitting beside the tuna dip.

"Wolf," said Blade, "can you make that call for us? Count Nefarious and I need to find the restroom, *if you know what I mean.* Is that okay, Mr. Corben?"

"Oh, yes. Of course. Come boys, I'll show you where it is."

Wolf grumbled as they left, and took the carrot stick the Bride of Frankenstein offered him.

Mr. Corben led the other two through the huge living room. The boys made sure to hide their faces when they passed Rhett and Scarlett, whom they recognized instantly. This was going to be hard enough without the Bursts asking questions. They turned a corner behind Mr. Corben.

"Okay, boys. Here you go. See you back in the kitchen," he said, and walked off.

Blade and Count Nefarious looked at each other, then snuck back around the corner and crept up the stairs, believing they had left everyone downstairs.

They couldn't have known something awaited them on the second floor.

15

"Do you see anything?" Blade whispered to the Count, who was going through the Corbens' master bedroom closet.

"No. I don't think this stupid thing exists," replied the Count. "I've dug through all of their personal belongings, but I haven't seen any doll."

"I'll look in another room," said Blade. "It has to be here."

He crept across the hallway into the next room, hoping that Mr. Corben wouldn't catch on to their disappearance too soon. He opened the door to a tiny exercise room with a closet, and proceeded to look around. Finding nothing in the room, he looked in the closet.

Flipping on the light, he eyed every inch of the storage space, until he felt a loose floorboard under his shoe.

He pulled up the carpet.

When he did, he found a perfectly-cut square floorboard that he could lift out. When he did, he noticed something wrapped in cloth. He unwrapped it, and there she was.

Floris DeDoris.

The ugliest doll he'd ever seen.

Red yarn hair. Dirty torn skin made of rags. A stained blue dress. Black button eyes and a stitched smile.

Oh yeah, this would be a lot of fun to play with, Blade thought, holding it up to his face. *I can see why you're her favorite.* Then he snickered, "You're the ugliest doll I've ever seen."

The doll turned its head, reared back its arm, and punched Blade right in the nose.

Shocked and hurt, Blade dropped Floris DeDoris and slid away from her, holding his sneezer.

The doll lay on the floor convulsing. It groaned and kicked its legs in the air—*and seemed to be growing.*

Count Nefarious walked in and froze. Blade couldn't move, he was so stricken with fear.

In a split second, the doll had reached the size of a small child—and continued to grow. It made awful sounds. Sounds like muscles squishing together and rubber being stretched. A constant low growl came from the doll's mouth—a slit under the nose that moved on its own.

Margot, who now possessed the Floris DeDoris doll, demanded . . .

"WHERE . . . IS . . . LILLIAN?"

💀 💀 💀

"Where do we find her?" Waylon asked as they pulled up beside the palace.

Manny the Friendly Person turned and pointed his head at a small curtain on the side of the grand cardboard structure.

"You see that cloth? That's the way in. But you'll have to go alone."

"Why?" Waylon asked, getting scared.

"Well, for one, I'm too big to fit through that tiny hole. Two, you've been inside that place. It's nothing but ductways, and I've got no hands to crawl with. Sorry, pal. This is where Fashion Bug and I part ways with you."

Waylon gulped, "What do you think my

chances are of actually finding her in that maze?"

"If you don't find her, she'll find you. There's no in-between. Now, uh, prepare for passenger eject!" ordered Manny the Friendly Person, as Fashion Bug's seat suddenly sprang up and popped Waylon into the air. He landed on his feet.

"Remember! If you find her, half the battle's won!" Manny cried as he and Fashion Bug drove away.

How's that for gratitude? Waylon thought. *Not even a 'thank you' for risking my life! Stupid, self-absorbed, ungrateful, poltergeist memories . . .*

He looked down at the soft ground into which his feet seemed to be sinking. Blue shag carpet. As far as his eyes could see, the ground was covered with the same blue shag carpet his father had ripped up from Waylon's own closet and replaced many years ago. Waylon trudged up the surreal landscape to the curtain to which Manny had pointed. He lifted the cloth to see a narrow dark hole that appeared to have no end. Against the advice of every intelligent voice screaming in his head, Waylon took a deep breath and climbed in.

At first, he barely had room to crawl, but the tunnel eventually got wider—though Waylon could still see no light at the end. After a few more feet, he could've sworn he heard something hissing.

"WAYLON, WE THOUGHT YOU'D NEVER COME BACK ..."

His heart stopped. That voice. He'd heard that voice before. He knew the hissing, and he knew what he would see when he turned around, though he prayed he was wrong.

He wasn't.

As Waylon slowly glanced over his shoulder, he saw the monster from his nightmares. The monster that chased him every time he closed his eyes. The monster from the woods.

Its eyes glowed in the darkness. Waylon could see it there, crammed into the tiny space, its oily scaled body rubbing against the walls. Its mouth opening and closing, biting the air with its teeth.

It was there, twenty yards behind him.

"REMEMBER ME?" it asked.

Waylon did remember, and he screamed.

16

Waylon crawled frantically through the flimsy tunnel, pushing and kicking, moving faster as the lizard monster came after him. Although it was as big as Waylon, it wasn't confined to just the floor of the tunnel. It scurried through the passage, climbing on the walls *and* ceiling to further its chase.

Waylon couldn't scream anymore. He couldn't think anymore. All he could do was breath hard and try to stay alive! Sweat ran into his eyes and blurred his vision. He never even saw the hole . . .

He fell, dropping like a laundry bag through a chute and bouncing off the walls and curves. A long descent. He actually spun around in freefall and saw the lizard in hot pursuit, shimmying down the ductway after him.

Waylon found his voice again and screamed the rest of the way down—until the tunnel took a sharp sideways turn. It dispensed him onto the floor of a new ductway, slamming him back-first against the sidewall.

Waylon saw the lizard land and fly right at him.

Either on guts, reflex, or the sheer will to survive, Waylon found his fist—and drove it right into the face of the oncoming creature.

The roundhouse punch stunned the monster, knocking it backwards and giving Waylon a chance to get to his feet.

This tunnel was large enough for him to actually stand in . . . *and run*. Waylon tore away as the dazed monster got to its feet and came after him. He felt the cardboard shake under his feet. Shaking like crazy. Just as the lizard got closer, Waylon saw another opening in one of the walls. It would be a high jump, but he could possibly make it. With the entire cardboard structure rumbling violently under his feet, Waylon leapt—*and managed to grab the edge of the opening*.

As he climbed up the shaking walls, the lizard grabbed his feet.

"RUNNING AWAY AGAIN, WAYLON?" it hissed.

Waylon strained, pulled one of his feet loose, and kicked the lizard square in the head. Once. Twice. Three times. When the rumbling reached full quake, the lizard let go—unable to hold on.

And the Blanket rolled through.

Roaring around the corner, it crashed through tunnelway—

The lizard only had time to gasp before the patchwork powerhouse exploded into the passageway and washed over him.

The thundering turbulence almost loosened Waylon's grip, but he held on enough to pull himself into the opening and out of the tunnelway as the Blanket crashed through.

Once through the hole, Waylon fell. There was nothing to grab on to, everything was pitch black—and all he could do was fall . . .

💀 💀 💀

"HELP ME!" Blade screamed as he bounded down Mr. Corben's stairway. Count Nefarious was one leap behind him. Both were screaming as if they were insane. The party-goers looked up in terror as they saw a giant raggedy thing crash down the stairs after them—demanding . . .

"TAKE ME TO LILLIAN! TELL ME WHERE SHE IS HIDING!"

The boys didn't answer her. Instead, they blew through the screaming crowd and back into the kitchen where Wolf had his ear to the phone.

"IT'S ABOUT TIME! *Hey, I just ordered a pizza . . .*"

"RUN!!" yelled Blade and Count Nefarious as they tore through the kitchen. Wolf didn't have a chance to ask anything before he saw the huge, torn, black-eyed raggedy face coming his way.

He didn't even have a chance to scream.

The Terrible Three blasted into the garage. They climbed over the truck, and went for the door on the other side—which would lead them out of there.

"OPEN IT! OPEN IT! IT'LL TAKE US BACK TO WAYLON'S!" Wolf yelled. Blade opened it.

The only thing on the other side was the backyard.

"FORGET IT! JUST GO! GO!" Wolf screamed, and Blade went through just as Floris

DeDoris exploded through the garage and slammed into the truck. Wolf flew out the door. Count Nefarious barely slipped out before the truck crashed into the sidewall.

The Terrible Three got to their feet. Before Wolf could give the command to run Waylon's house, he saw Count Nefarious and Blade already heading that way.

Behind him, the doorway he'd just come through ripped wide open and Floris DeDoris came through.

Wolf jetted after the others. Now it was a footrace.

17

"FASTER! SHE'S STILL BEHIND US!" Wolf cried as they tore down the street. Looking behind him, he could see the giant raggedy doll racing after them as it passed under the street lights. It wasn't stopping—and it was very fast.

"JUST ONE MORE BLOCK!" cried Count Nefarious, overtaking the slower Blade.

A car drove past them as they ran. When its headlights encountered Floris DeDoris in hot pursuit, it ran off the road and into some nearby shrubbery.

Panicking, Blade looked back and saw the thing still coming. Relentlessly chasing them until it caught them or until . . .

"THERE IT IS!" Count Nefarious cried as they turned a wide corner and saw Waylon's house. None of the lights were on.

As the three ran for the front yard, a car pulled in front of them.

Mr. Wincott.

The Terrible Three came to a quick halt—saving them from crashing into the car.

"WHAT'S GOING ON HERE?" Mr. Wincott screamed.

Then he saw the hulking thing that was chasing them.

The boys clambered over the hood of the car just as Floris DeDoris reached it—bounding into the air and then crashing down on the car's front end. Mr. Wincott's seat actually sprang up when the monster smashed the car's engine to the ground.

The Terrible Three bolted through the yard and up to the front door with Floris DeDoris right on their heels.

When they blasted through the door, a surprise awaited them.

There was no floor.

"OH, NO! BOYS, WATCH OUT!" Mrs. Wincott cried from her seat on the hovering stairwell at the other end of the room.

But the boys had been coming too quickly. They fell forward.

With lightning-fast reflexes, Count Nefarious gripped onto the handle of the swinging door. As he fell, Blade grabbed the Count's ankles. And as he passed them, Wolf roped his arms around Blade's plump legs.

They hung there, just as the unstoppable Margot crashed through the doorway . . . *and dropped.*

The boys hung from the doorknob, not taking their eyes off of the monster doll as it plummeted into the darkness.

No one said a word. No one could, until a frazzled Mr. Wincott appeared at the door and saw his wife sitting on the stairs, hovering over the void.

He could think of nothing to say but, "I have your medicine. Do you want it now?"

☠ ☠ ☠

"*No,*" Waylon muttered, as if he could hear the ground rush towards him.

He hit hard, landing on a thicker version of the blue shag carpeting he'd seen before.

He lay there for a second, astounded that he was still alive. Then he got to his feet and looked around.

He was in another tunnel, the largest one he'd seen. But at the end of this one there was light—something bright and golden, shining in the darkness.

He walked toward it. The air became warmer with every step he took, and when he entered the glow, he felt so comfortable he didn't want to leave. When he came through the glow, he marveled at the sight before him.

A room made of pure gold.

Golden floor. Golden columns. Even a golden fountain in the center of a vast royal dome. Diamond chandeliers hung from a ceiling that was high enough for an enclosed stadium. What's more, Waylon could see doves passing each other in the air as they flew overhead.

On the other side of the grand palace, he saw what looked like a throne (made of gold, of course). It sat in front of a massive twenty-foot-tall door with sparkling diamond trim. Someone was lounging on the throne, waiting for Waylon to approach.

It was deathly silent as he walked closer. He tried to get a good look at who watched him from the royal chair, but the doves kept swooping down in front of him. He didn't discover who it was until he was almost sitting in the chair himself.

"Bonnie . . .?" he said, amazed.

"Hi, Waylon," she said, then made a motion to the grandeur around them. "Pretty rad, huh?"

"Are you okay?" he asked, still nervous about the vast open space around him. It felt like a coliseum.

"Waylon, what do you think? Do you see this place?" she asked, motioning once again to the palace-like room. "She gave this to me, Waylon. All of this is mine!"

"All of this is yours? How?" he asked.

Bonnie grinned and scooped some grapes out of a bowl which sat next to her throne.

"I protect her now. All I have to do is make sure no one opens that door," she said, pointing to the towering passage a few feet behind the throne.

"What's behind it?" he asked.

"My servants told me that it's not only the way to find Lillian, but it's also how to find many other things. It could be a doorway to salvation, or a doorway to doom."

Waylon had found his missing poltergeist.

"Listen, I've discovered something. Lillian's going to keep haunting my house until I find her and convince her to stop. Plus, she's misusing all of the images she's pulled from her childhood memories. I've talked to them, and they want to be set free."

"They want to be set free? That's a hoot. Where's the Blanket going to go from here? Does it think it'll actually cover the *President's* feet someday? And you're telling me that some kid will want to go to sleep at night and dream of this melted ugly G.I. Joan? Puh-lease. Where else are these childhood memories going to exist if they're not here with Lillian and me?"

"I'll remember them," said Waylon. "I'll remember them and think about them. That's gotta be better than this."

"*You'll* think about them, Waylon? Even the monsters?" Bonnie asked in an unbelieving tone.

Waylon nodded, "Even the monsters."

Bonnie stopped eating her grapes and dropped them into the bowl. She stood up and looked Waylon straight in the eye.

"Well, I'm afraid I can't let you open that door. I've dreamt of living in a place like this my whole life, Waylon. I'm not giving it up now that I have it. So, if you want to go through that door, prepare to fight for it."

"Bonnie, listen to me. There's more to this than you know. Lillian is not the only poltergeist. There's another one named Margot. She's bigger than Lillian. She used to bully Lillian. And if she ever finds this place, she'll be too much for you to handle!"

"Waylon, all you're worried about is your stupid house and your stupid room! That's why you're saying all of this stuff! Listen, don't worry! Once Lillian gets Floris DeDoris back, we're out of here! She only wants her doll back—that's all!"

"That's what I'm trying to tell you! Margot's staying with the doll because she can't find Lillian and she knows Lillian'll come looking for it! Floris DeDoris is a trap, she's—"

"HEEEEEEERRRRRRRRREEEEEE."

The voice shook the golden foundations around them. Waylon and Bonnie froze, their eyes scanning . . .

Then, in the tunnel from which Waylon

had come, something appeared. It came out of
the darkness and into the light. It that looked
like a doll. A raggedy doll . . .

**"I'VE FOUND YOU, LILLIAN. I'VE FINAL-
LY FOUND YOU AGAIN! NOW I'LL PUT
YOU IN THE AFTERWORLD
WHERE YOU BELONG . . ."**

"What in the world . . .?" Bonnie muttered, and stood up.

Waylon held her back.

"MARGOT."

18

The canvas-covered monster came into the light. The dingy gridwork of its face appeared first, one eye pulled and hanging, its mouth ripped wide with a drooping curl of material flapping as it moved. Its burnt-red twine hair hung from its head like a mop, except for the spots where it had been ripped away. When it came into full view, its lumbering, brown, cloth body heaved in fury. Stuffing fell to the floor from small rips in its stitched skin, but it didn't seem to notice.

Margot had finally found what she was looking for.

"LILLIAN! I KNOW YOU'RE BEHIND THAT DOOR, LILLIAN."

"Oh my gosh, Waylon. I've got to stop her," Bonnie said. "*How* am I going to stop her?"

Waylon shook his head, unable to offer any suggestions.

Margot started toward them, her arms dragging on the floor at her sides.

"I've got to call for reinforcements," said Bonnie, thrusting her hands into her pockets.

"Reinforcements? What are you talking about?"

"More lizard-creatures! She copied them from the drawings she saw on your wall! I'll get the Blanket, too, if I can find that stupid whistle!"

"Whistle?"

"Yeah, my 'call to arms' whistle. I stuck it in one of these pockets somewhere . . . oh, yeah, my shirt pocket—"

Just as Bonnie got the whistle into her hand, Margot was upon them.

One of her huge arms knocked Waylon to the floor. With the other, she lifted Bonnie into the air, causing her to drop the whistle.

"LILLIAN CANNOT HIDE FROM ME!"

"PUT A SOCK IN IT!" Bonnie screamed, and kicked off Margot's other button eye.

Waylon got to his feet and rushed at the doll monster, grabbing one of its legs and ripping into it. Margot kicked him into the air, and when he landed on his back, the air left his lungs.

Bonnie saw Waylon go down and growled in anger. With her nails, she started tearing into Margot's doll-skin. She pulled out chunk after chunk of cotton stuffing, until Margot took her other hand and smacked her in the head. Dazed, Bonnie didn't have a chance to react as Margot held her to her rippped-open mouth and dropped her in.

"NO!" Waylon screamed in horror as he got to his feet. *She did it. She really did it!*

Bonnie was gone!

"YOU EVIL—"

Waylon rushed at Margot without thinking. Before he reached the terrible creature, it raised its monstrous fist into the air and brought it crashing down on the back of Waylon's shoulders.

He folded like a chair and dropped to the ground.

Silently, Margot turned around and walked to the door. Gripping the golden handle with her canvas mitts, she pulled it open and looked at what lay on the other side.

19

"It can't be," Margot uttered. **"IT CAN'T BE!"**

She backed up, gazing through the doorway at the gigantic face of Lillian, whose angered expression filled the entire opening. Seething, she peered down at her former doll, now possessed by a bully who had pushed her too far.

"HELLO, MARGOT," Lillian boomed.

Margot continued to back away, trembling at the sight before her.

"You . . . you've gotten bigger," Margot muttered shakingly.

"I'm fed up with this. You've chased me and bullied me for a very long time—but now it's over. You've invaded the last place I had to go, so now the only thing I can do is fight you. You're never going to bully me again, Margot."

"No. NOOO!" Margot screamed, shocked by Lillian's immense power. Thoughts of retaliation didn't occur to her. She felt only fear. "NOOOO!" she screamed again and before the giant could make good on her threat, Margot ran forward and slammed the door shut. She immediately ran back—terrified of what Lillian might do next.

Seconds passed.

Nothing happened.

Margot quit shaking. It slowly dawned on her that there would be no answer from Lillian.

"SHE'S STILL SCARED! SHE'S STILL TERRIFIED OF ME! SHE WON'T EVEN COME OUT HERE AND FACE ME HERSELF!"

Triumphant, she spun around to see Waylon feebly get to his feet. A grin crept across her face. Before she faced Lillian again, she would crush her foe's foot soldiers.

"DID YOU HEAR ME?" Margot demanded from Waylon. "LILLIAN DOESN'T HAVE THE GUTS TO COME OUT HERE AND FIGHT!"

Waylon stood in the middle of the gigantic room and looked straight into Margot's horrible face. He seemed as though he might fall over, then . . .

"No. That's not it. She just left you up to me," he said, then brought Bonnie's whistle up to his lips and blew.

At first there was silence. Margot turned to pounce, but stopped when she looked at the tunnel which she had entered . . .

. . . *Hundreds of red eyes glowing in the darkness.*

"No . . ." she squeaked.

"Yes," affirmed Waylon.

And then, in they came.

A stampeding herd of lizard-creatures, all moving to attack one common enemy. They streamed by Waylon, an ocean of bouncing green scaly heads, and rushed at Margot before she could turn and run.

They jumped on top of her and clawed at her fighting cloth form. Soon she was covered in ripping, biting lizards. She couldn't get away.

"NO! NOOOOOOO!"

Waylon stood back, privately cheering at first, but he quickly grew sickened.

"OKAY! BACK OFF!" he shouted. **"BACK OFF!"**

The lizards continued their feast.

"BACK OFF, I SAID!" Waylon yelled, and blew the whistle again.

The creatures ceased their attack and slowly climbed off the mutilated doll.

Waylon slowly walked over to it and saw the tears running down its face. It still had enough life in it to speak . . .

"I . . . I'm sorry—please . . . don't hurt me anymore . . . I won't do it again . . . It's over—my hunt's over . . . I won't bother Lillian again . . . "

The pitiful pleas of a bully who's been shown the light. It made Waylon's stomach turn. He couldn't help thinking that, at one time, it could've been him lying there begging the forgiveness of a kid he once thought weak. His actions in the past had come back to haunt him, literally.

A glow emanated from Margot's torn center, growing brighter until . . . a ball of light emerged.

It hovered in the air for a moment, reflecting in Waylon's eyes. He could look into it. *He could actually look into it!* It seemed to say goodbye, then floated upwards, disappearing through the ceiling.

Waylon stood breathless for a second, then heard something rumbling under the cottony corpse that was once Margot.

He saw a huge clump of stuffing rise, and then fall away. Under it lay a groaning Bonnie.

"BONNIE!" Waylon cried. "YOU'RE ALL RIGHT!"

"Of course I'm all right," she moaned. "Dolls don't have digestive tracts."

"I—I just didn't know! It's over Bonnie! Margot's gone!"

"Gone? How?" Bonnie asked, shakily getting to her feet and pulling the stuffing out of her ears.

"Well, me and the guys took care of her," he said, nervously motioning to the army of lizard-creatures that surrounded them. "Of course, this all happened after she opened the door and—"

"THE DOOR!" Bonnie cried, looking back at the open entrance. "LILLIAN! IS SHE OKAY?"

"I don't know," said Waylon. "Why don't we find out?"

20

The two of them approached the open door, and peered inside.

There was no huge head—no angry eyes staring back at them.

Bonnie squinted.

"Is that . . .?"

"I can't tell," Waylon said.

The room on the other side of the door seemed to go on forever. And in the distance, something glowed. It looked like a person.

They walked through the door.

It was dark, but there was enough light for them to see where they were going.

Waylon noticed that the floor beneath turned to blue shag carpet once again. The ceiling lowered as they went, and it was soon apparent that the dark room narrowed. It wasn't at all the size the large door had implied. In fact, the farther they went in, the more normal-sized the room became until finally, it almost felt . . . cramped.

But what kept them focused, what they had set their eyes on from the very beginning, was the tiny blue glow at the other end. As they drew closer, they both realized who they were approaching. It sat in a huddled mass at their feet. Although they already knew in their hearts what is was, they still had to ask . . .

"Lillian?" asked Bonnie.

On the floor in front of them, curled in a corner, was a little girl of about seven. Her whole body had a blue cast as well as a faint glow. Upon hearing the name, she looked up at them with sad eyes, and nodded.

"Lillian, where are we?" Waylon asked in a soft voice. Then the cramped room became a little more visible, but still looked dark. Lonely.

Then Waylon uttered . . .

"This . . . this looks like my closet."

Someone approached them from behind.

Waylon and Bonnie spun around, expecting to see a doll-headed horror moving in to attack.

What they saw was Manny the Friendly Person.

"It *is* your closet, kiddo," he said. "Your closet is Lillian's sanctuary. It's where she hid from the things that frightened her most."

"Margot . . ." said Bonnie.

"Especially Margot. But when that monster invaded this place—the best hiding place she had ever had—Lillian had to fight back. It was the bravest thing she's ever done. It took a lot out of her."

"This was her hiding place?" asked Waylon.

"Yeah," replied Manny. "She would hide in this closet and play with her toys to forget about the awful outside world where bullies terrorized her and her parents ignored her."

"Her parents . . . ?" asked Waylon.

"Workhorses, they were. Never had a lot of time to spend with her. Her mom tried—even took her to work with her sometimes. When we came back, that's the first place Lillian looked. But her mom didn't work there anymore . . . "

"Didn't she have any friends?" Bonnie asked.

"No one wanted to be her friend, what with Margot beating her up every day and taking her toys. The kids just let the bully torment her until that last day when . . . "

Lillian covered her ears, not wanting to hear the words.

"We know, Manny. We know what happened," said Waylon.

Bonnie bent down to try and comfort the little girl. When she saw Lillian's face, something clicked in her head.

"Waylon, I've seen her before. I saw her on your videotape. She was following you around the rooms today before I arrived."

Manny the Friendly Person grinned.

"I think she feels a kind of kinship with Fraidy Boy. Even though she was confused as to why someone else was in her room, she noticed that they shared a lot of feelings. Neither of them like the outdoors. Both of them would rather live in their rooms. And neither of them really have friends . . ."

"That's not true," Waylon snapped, starting to get defensive. "I've got friends! I've got lots of them, like . . .uh . . well, there's . . ."

"Me," Bonnie said.

"YEAH. Bonnie. Bonnie's my friend," Waylon said, and then glanced down at Lillian, whose sad look wouldn't disappear.

"And Lillian, too. Lillian can be my friend."

Lillian looked up at him and smiled.

"Well, all this cutesy-coo is going to make this Friendly Person sick. I'm getting out of here as soon as I ask Miss Lillian a question . . . *Miss Lillian,* will you let us go?"

Lillian looked at him, pretending she didn't understand the question.

"Will you let us go? Me, Fashion Bug, Blanket, G.I. Joan, the Space Ghoul, and even the remains of Margot/Floris DeDoris out there . . . will you let us go? We, the memories, have been with you for so long now, and we're the *same old memories*. It seems we're the only ones you have and that's not fair to us. It's stressful. We're asking you—no, begging you—*gather some new memories*. Please give us a much deserved break! We'll be there whenever you want us, we really will, but right now we're just overworked! Can you find it in your heart to give us a rest?"

Lillian gazed at him, unsure as to how to answer.

Bonnie didn't understand.

"I don't get it? If all of these manifestations are Lillian's *only* cherished memories, how can she hope to replace them?"

Waylon bent down to meet Lillian eye-to-eye.

"I think I know," he said.

And Lillian smiled. She knew, too.

Then suddenly Manny disappeared, and a magnificent light filled the room. It grew until the closet completely disappeared.

And for the first time in a long time, Waylon felt safe. As the light grew brighter, he, along with Bonnie and Lillian, disappeared into it.

21

Without warning, the Burst home returned to normal. Everything was reversed. At least, everything *Lillian* had done was reversed. The mess that Wolf, Blade, and Count Nefarious had made still lay strewn on the floor.

None of them were moving too quickly to clean it up, however. The Terrible Three, along with Mr. Wincott, lay in a heap on the couch, still trying to comprehend everything they'd seen in the last few hours. Mr. Wincott had even taken some of his wife's nerve medication. It had relaxed him, and he was totally at peace when a much disheveled Rhett and Scarlett appeared at the door.

"What? What's going on here?" asked Mr. Burst, throwing his hat toward the hat rack but missing it since it was lying on the floor. Then he saw the three kids on his couch.

"YOU! THE LITTLE RUFFIANS WHO RUINED THE CORBENS' PARTY! YOU DECIDED TO VISIT THE WHOLE NEIGHBORHOOD, EH? WELL, I HAVEN'T GOTTEN ANYONE IN A HEADLOCK IN QUITE A WHILE, BUT—"

The three boys were off the couch and out the front door, slamming it shut before Mr. Burst could make another move.

Mr. Wincott, totally useless by now, looked up at the couple and smiled.

"Mr. Wincott?" Mrs. Burst began to question him as Mrs. Wincott emerged from the kitchen holding a shaky cup of tea.

"Mrs. Wincott?" Mrs. Burst asked again. "Wh—What happened here? Where are Bonnie and Waylon?"

Mrs. Wincott almost began her first attempt at answering such a tricky question, but the door behind the Bursts suddenly creaked open. Rhett and Scarlett whipped around to see Waylon and Bonnie standing in the doorway.

They glared at Waylon in amazement.

"WAYLON? YOU WERE . . . OUTSIDE?"

Waylon couldn't help but grin.

"Yeah, I'm sorry we scared you guys. I just felt like I needed some fresh air!"

Waylon's dad smiled, grabbed Bonnie's hand, and shook it.

"Congratulations. You've done something two parents, ten doctors, and twenty other sitters failed to do—get my pale son outside—even if it *was* at night! Do you think you could get him out in the sun next time?"

"Well," said Bonnie, grinning at Waylon. "I can try . . ."

22

The sun shone down on Waylon and Bonnie as they lay on lawn chairs in the Bursts' front yard, soaking up the rays. It was the brightest day either one of them could remember. Waylon's pale skin looked dark only in comparison to the vanilla ice cream cone he was casually licking while trying to look cool in his shades. Bonnie slurped down the last of her cola and then turned to Waylon.

"I think you're getting burnt," she said.

Waylon shot up and looked at his arms.

"No way," he said.

Bonnie found the final drop of cola with her straw before asking, "Are you ready to go in?"

"I don't know. It's so noisy in there. Dad's putting a new addition on the house. Why don't you go in and live there in my stead. I'll stay out here and tan."

"Thanks, but no thanks. I've had it with big houses. I'm going to build my own cottage someday—*with no doors or closets,* of course. That way, my odds on being haunted are very low. *Now c'mon*—we've been at this for an hour. And Mrs. Wincott wanted us to come over for lunch."

"Poltergeists, poltergeists, poltergeists. That's all she ever wants to talk about when she sees us. I wish she'd just let it rest . . ."

"Well, are you ready?" Bonnie asked again.

"Yeah. Let's go," said Waylon, and the two packed up their gear and walked to Waylon's front door.

Waylon turned the knob, and both of them went through the doorway . . .

. . . And stepped right out of Waylon's closet into his room.

Lillian lay on his bed, reading one of his poltergeist books and correcting the parts with which she didn't agree.

"Thanks for the manifestation, Lillian," said Waylon. "That was great! Bonnie actually thinks I got some sun!"

Lillian shook her head in disbelief.

Then Waylon's face turned serious.

"Um, Bonnie's actually talked me into going outside," he announced. "We're going over to Mrs. Wincott's for lunch."

Lillian looked up at him in surprise.

"Yeah, she won't leave us alone! All she ever wants to talk about are poltergeists . . ."

Lillian frowned. Waylon hadn't told her he was leaving . . . *what would she do there alone?*

Then, as Waylon and Bonnie were halfway out the door, Waylon popped his head back in and noticed his poltergeist friend was still sitting on the bed.

"HEY! WHAT ARE YOU WAITING FOR?" asked Waylon. "ARE YOU COMING OR NOT?"

Lillian's face instantly lit up. She bounded off the bed and joined her two friends for adventures from which she was sure she would collect many great memories.

The three of them left the room, off to teach Mrs. Wincott more than she ever wanted to know about poltergeists . . .

And the door closed.

About the Authors

Marty M. Engle and **Johnny Ray Barnes Jr.**, graduates of the Art Institute of Atlanta, are the creators, writers, designers and illustrators of the **Strange Matter™** series and the **Strange Matter™ World Wide Web page.**

Their interests and expertise range from state of the art 3-D computer graphics and interactive multi-media, to books and scripts (television and motion picture).

Marty lives in La Jolla, California with his wife Jana and twin terror pets, Polly and Oreo.

Johnny Ray lives in Tierrasanta, California and spends every free moment with his wife Meredith.

BUILD YOUR OWN HAUNTED LIBRARY

For more stories and facts on poltergeists and other types of ghosts, be sure to read:

☠ **Hans Holzer's Haunted America** - Professor Holzer records his investigations of the paranormal over some thirty states.

☠ **Gazetteer of British, Scottish & Irish Ghosts** by Peter Underwood - A comprehensive reference book and guide to the ghost population of the British Isles. *Very* creepy stories!

☠ **ESP, Hauntings, and Poltergeists** by Loyd Aurbach - A professional paraphsychologist's guide to ghosts, hauntings, and paranormal research.

FOR BRAVE READERS EVERYWHERE!

And now
an exciting preview
of the next

#21 Under Wraps

by Marty M. Engle

1

Ten-year-old Albert Whitley's glasses slid down his nose and hung precariously on his sweat-soaked face.

He would have pushed them back up but his arms were plastered to his sides.

Somewhere in his mind, amid the shrieking and screaming, the thought occurred to him to run. Fear, however, froze him in place making movement impossible—except for his eyes. He stood stone-still, terrified, as his eyes rolled and darted about the dark, dreary chamber, watching the bobbing blurry faces of his tormentors. They laughed and sneered, passing the ends of long white strips to each other as they continued their ghastly work.

He bit his trembling lower lip and shut his eyes tightly. His nerves collapsed with a low moan. He felt the white strips tighten around his legs, wrap around his knees, and wind their way up his body like a snake—joining three previous layers, guided by two pairs of eager, merciless hands.

"Don't move. You'll only make it harder on yourself," an icy voice croaked, inches from his face.

"Yeah, Whitley. Move and we'll kill you," another growled in his ear.

A third, chilling, emotionless voice, echoed from the darkest corner of the chamber, floating through the dank air.

"Faster, gentlemen, FASTER! We're running out of time. Finish him now!"

Albert felt his throbbing heart swell into his throat, choking off his breath. The strips of white criss-crossed his body faster, cocooning him, wrapping around his back and across his chest, passed along with ever-increasing speed by his two tormentors.

"Yes," the third voice cried with new-found enthusiasm. "Yes! That's it! That's fine. His head. Don't forget his head."

A strip crossed his gaping mouth, gagging him, as his tormentors laughed. Another wound around the back of his head and across his nose. He felt his glasses being plucked from his face as a final strip was pulled across his tightly-shut eyes.

"Tear a single strip and we'll pound your face, got me? We'll be watching, too," the first voice growled.

"Oh, and enjoy the exhibit, mummy-boy," the cruelest voice laughed.

He heard their eerie laughter disappear into the hall as the bathroom door closed behind them.

Albert Whitley didn't move a muscle. He stood in front of the wide mirror and pale white sinks where his tormentors had placed him before they began. Although he couldn't see, he could hear the water drips echoing off the pale-green tile walls. And his own gurgling moan.

His brain seethed with fury and embarrassment. *Where was his friend? If Jon was here, he would've stopped them.*

He would've saved me.

"JON!" the sweet but exasperated voice called from the front door. "JON! DO YOU PLAN ON EATING TODAY?"

Jonathan Drake sprinted back up the

steps to the front porch of his two-story home and grabbed the blue canvas lunch bag from his mother's hand.

He smiled and waved as he ran back down to the driveway. "Thanks, Mom! Gotta hurry! Albert and Nate are waiting for me!"

Jon jumped onto his bike and sailed down the driveway to his tree-lined street.

"JONATHAN DRAKE! PLEASE BE CAREFUL!" his mother called behind him. "TRY NOT TO GET INTO ANY TROUBLE TODAY!"

Jon honked his bike horn in reply.

The trees towered above him with bright-orange, yellow, and brown leaves. As was the case every October, the trees of Bentley Street painted the sky like a fireworks display. Their long shadows played across the sidewalk as Jon steered his bike through the alternating ribbons of light and shade.

"This is gonna be a great day!" he cried, the damp, cool morning air rushing across his face. The clicking and clacking of his bicycle chain filled his ears with joy. His favorite denim jacket still felt warm from the dryer, and for once, his heart filled with excitement at the thought of going to school.

The blast of a car horn and the loud squeal of brakes cut his bliss short. He had swerved sharply across the street—without looking first.

"Sorry, Mr. Sanders!" he yelled, waving at the man shaking his head in the sedan.

Keep your mind on the road, Jon, he thought to himself, turning down Sycamore Street. *The exhibit will be there, but you won't if you keep riding like that.*

He pedalled faster and popped a wheelie, flying toward the end of the cul-de-sac where he would cut through the Whites' backyard—part of his emergency route to Fairfield Junior High.

Almost there, he thought.

Jon's excitement was shared by most of the students of Fairfield Junior High that day. It was the day of the special exhibit in the school gymnasium. A rare treat in the spirt of Halloween—with educational value, of course.

A mummy exhibit.

With *real* mummies.

Maybe I'll be the first one there, Jon thought. *Nah. What am I thinking? Nate's probably already waiting at the door.*

Nate stood at the large light-brown door, pushed a strand of long red hair from his face, and anxiously peered through the small, wire-mesh-lined window.

No mummies . . . yet, he thought.

He lost track of how long he'd been standing there. Since this was the coolest thing to ever come to the school, he wanted to be the first to catch a glimpse.

Crates and boxes of all sizes sat on the polished gym floor. The workmen, dressed in dirty white jumpsuits, busily constructed a maze of black sectional walls and began hanging mounted photographs, illustrations, and descriptions on each.

The mummies must be in the crates, Nate thought, craning his neck to see.

Then he noticed the tall, strange man in the long dark-red robe. He was bent over a glass case near the center of the room and seemed to be intently studying whatever was inside. From the hallway, Nate couldn't make out exactly what was in the case—no matter how hard he craned his neck or darted his head.

He was so busy peering through the window, he failed to notice the trembling hand rising up behind him—*easing toward his neck.*

STRANGE MATTER™

Order now or take this page to your local bookstore!

Please send me the books I have checked above. I am enclosing $_____ (please add $2.00 to cover shipping and handling). Send check or money order to Montage Publications, 9808 Waples Street, San Diego, California 92121 - no cash or C.O.D.'s please.

NAME _____ AGE_____

ADDRESS_____

CITY_____ STATE _____ ZIP _____

Please allow four to six weeks for delivery. Offer good in the U.S. only. Sorry, mail orders are not available to residents of Canada. Prices subject to change.

JOIN THE FORCES!

STRANGERS™

An incredible new club exclusively for readers of Strange Matter™

To receive exclusive information on joining this *strange* new organization, simply fill out the slip below and mail to:

STRANGE MATTER™ INFO •Front Line Art Publishing • 9808 Waples St. • San Diego, California 92121

Name _____ Age _____

Address _____

City _____ State _____ Zip _____

How did you hear about Strange Matter™? _____

_____

What other series do you read? _____

_____

Where did you get this Strange Matter™ book? _____

_____

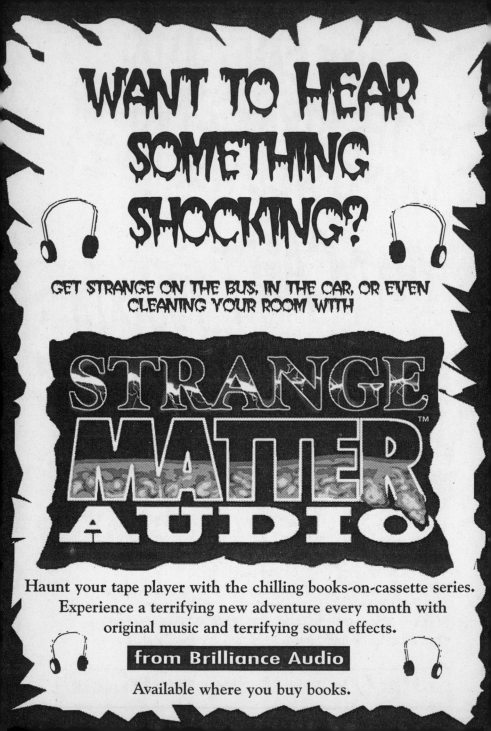